THE STAINLESS STEEL RAT
AND THE MISPLACED BATTLESHIP

Cover Image © Can Stock Photo Inc. / Catmando

Positronic Publishing
PO Box 632
Floyd VA 24091

ISBN 13: 978-1-5154-0237-4

First Positronic Publishing Edition
10 9 8 7 6 5 4 3 2 1

THE STAINLESS STEEL RAT
AND THE MISPLACED BATTLESHIP

by Harry Harrison

When it comes to picking locks and cracking safes I admit to no master. The door to Inskipp's private quarters had an old-fashioned tumbler drum that was easier to pick than my teeth. I must have gone through that door without breaking step. Quiet as I was though, Inskipp still heard me. The light came on and there he was sitting up in bed pointing a .75 caliber recoilless at my sternum.

"You should have more brains than that, diGriz," he snarled. "Creeping into my room at night! You could have been shot."

"No I couldn't," I told him, as he stowed the cannon back under his pillow. "A man with a curiosity bump as big as yours will always talk first and shoot later. And besides—none of this pussyfooting around in the dark would be necessary if your screen was open and I could have got a call through."

Inskipp yawned and poured himself a glass of water from the dispenser unit above the bed. "Just because I head the Special Corps, doesn't mean that I *am* the Special Corps," he said moistly while he drained the glass. "I have to sleep sometime. My screen is open only for emergency calls, not for every agent who needs his hand held."

"Meaning I am in the hand-holding category?" I asked with as much sweetness as I could.

"Put yourself in any category you please," he grumbled as he slumped down in the bed. "And also put yourself out into the hall and see me tomorrow during working hours."

He was at my mercy, really. He wanted sleep so much. And he was going to be wide awake so very soon.

"Do you know what this is?" I asked him, poking a large glossy pic under his long broken nose. One eye opened slowly.

"Big warship of some kind, looks like Empire lines. Now for the last time—go away!" he said.

"A very good guess for this late at night," I told him cheerily. "It is a late Empire battleship of the Warlord class. Undoubtedly one of the most truly efficient engines of destruction ever manufactured. Over a half mile of defensive screens and armament, that could probably turn any fleet existent today into fine radioactive ash—"

"Except for the fact that the last one was broken up for scrap over a thousand years ago," he mumbled.

I leaned over and put my lips close to his ear. So there would be no chance of misunderstanding. Speaking softly, but clearly.

"True, true," I said. "But wouldn't you be just a *little* bit interested if I was to tell you that one is being built today?"

Oh, it was beautiful to watch. The covers went one way and Inskipp went the other. In a single unfolding, in concerted motion he left the horizontal and recumbent and stood tensely vertical against the wall. Examining the pic of the battleship under the light. He apparently did not believe in pajama bottoms and it hurt me to see the goose-bumps rising on those thin shanks. But if the legs were thin, the voice was more than full enough to make up for the difference.

"Talk, blast you diGriz—*talk!*" he roared. "What is this nonsense about a battleship? Who's building it?"

I had my nail file out and was touching up a cuticle, holding it out for inspection before I said anything. From the corner of my eye I could see him getting purple about the face—but he kept quiet. I savored my small moment of power.

"Put diGriz in charge of the record room for a while, you said, that way he can learn the ropes. Burrowing around in century-old, dusty files will be just the thing for a free spirit like Slippery Jim diGriz. Teach him discipline. Show him what the Corps stands for. At the same time it will get the records in shape. They have been needing reorganization for quite a while."

Inskipp opened his mouth, made a choking noise, then closed it. He undoubtedly realized that any interruption would only lengthen my explanation, not shorten it. I smiled and nodded at his decision, then continued.

"So you thought you had me safely out of the way. Breaking my spirit under the guise of 'giving me a little background in the Corps' activities.' In this sense your plan failed. Something else happened instead. I nosed through the files and found them most interesting. Particularly the C & M setup—the Categorizer and Memory. That building full of machinery that takes in and digests news and reports from all the planets in the galaxy, indexes it to every category it can possibly relate, then files it. Great machine to work with. I had it digging out spaceship info for me, something I have always been interested in—"

"You should be," Inskipp interrupted rudely. "You've stolen enough of them in your time."

I gave him a hurt look and went on—slowly. "I won't bore you with all the details, since you seem impatient, but eventually I turned up this plan." He had it out of my fingers before it cleared my wallet.

"What are you getting at?" he mumbled as he ran his eyes over the blueprints. "This is an ordinary heavy-cargo and passenger job. It's no more a Warlord battleship than I am."

* * * * *

It is hard to curl your lips with contempt and talk at the same time, but I succeeded. "Of course. You don't expect them to file warship plans with the League Registry, do you? But, as I said, I know more than a little bit about ships. It seemed to me this thing was just too big for the use intended. Enough old ships are fuel-wasters, you don't have to build new ones to do that. This started me thinking and I punched for a complete list of ships that size that had been constructed in the past. You can imagine my surprise when, after three minutes of groaning, the C & M only produced six. One was built for self-sustaining colony attempt at the second galaxy. For all we know she is still on the way. The other five were all D-class colonizers, built during the Expansion when large populations were moved. Too big to be practical now.

"I was still teased, as I had no idea what a ship this large could be used for. So I removed the time interlock on the C & M and let it pick around through the entire history of space to see if it could find a comparison. It sure did. Right at the Golden Age of Empire expansion, the giant Warlord battleships. The machine even found a blueprint for me."

Inskipp grabbed again and began comparing the two prints. I leaned over his shoulder and pointed out the interesting parts.

"Notice—if the engine room specs are changed slightly to include this cargo hold, there is plenty of room for the brutes needed. This superstructure—obviously just tacked onto the plans—gets thrown away, and turrets take its place. The hulls are identical. A change here, a shift there, and the stodgy freighter becomes the fast battlewagon. These changes could be made during construction, then plans filed. By the time anyone in the League found out what was being built the ship would be finished and launched. Of course, this could all be coincidence—the plans of a newly built ship agreeing to six places with those of a ship built a thousand years ago. But if you think so, I will give you hundred-to-one odds you are wrong, any size bet you name."

I wasn't winning any sucker bets that night. Inskipp had led just as crooked a youth as I had, and needed no help in smelling a fishy deal. While he pulled on his clothes he shot questions at me.

"And the name of the peace-loving planet that is building this bad memory from the past?"

"Cittanuvo. Second planet of a B star in Corona Borealis. No other colonized planets in the system."

"Never heard of it," Inskipp said as we took the private drop chute to his office. "Which may be a good or a bad sign. Wouldn't be the first time trouble came from some out-of-the-way spot I never even knew existed."

With the automatic disregard for others of the truly dedicated, he pressed the scramble button on his desk. Very quickly sleepy-eyed clerks and assistants were bringing files and records. We went through them together.

Modesty prevented me from speaking first, but I had a very short wait before Inskipp reached the same conclusion I had. He hurled a folder the length of the room and scowled out at the harsh dawn light.

"The more I look at this thing," he said, "the fishier it gets. This planet seems to have no possible motive or use for a battleship. But they are building one—*that* I will swear on a stack of one thousand credit notes as high as this building. Yet what will they do with it when they have it built? They have an expanding culture, no unemployment, a surplus of heavy metals and ready markets for all they produce. No hereditary enemies, feuds or the like. If it wasn't for this battleship thing, I would call them an ideal League planet. I have to know more about them."

"I've already called the spaceport—in your name of course," I told him. "Ordered a fast courier ship. I'll leave within the hour."

"Aren't you getting a little ahead of yourself, diGriz," he said. Voice chill as the icecap. "I still give the orders and I'll tell you when you're ready for an independent command."

I was sweetness and light because a lot depended on his decision. "Just trying to help, chief, get things ready in case you wanted more info. And this isn't really an operation, just a reconnaissance. I can do that as well as any of the experienced operators. And it may give me the experience I need, so that some day, I, too, will be qualified to join the ranks...."

"All right," he said. "Stop shoveling it on while I can still breathe. Get out there. Find out what is going on. Then get back. Nothing else—and that's an order."

By the way he said it, I knew he thought there was little chance of its happening that way. Since my forced induction into the Corps six months earlier I had been stuck on this super-secret planetoid that was its headquarters and main base. I had very little sitting-down patience anyway, and it had been long since exhausted.

  * * * * *

It had been interesting at first. Particularly since up until the time I was drafted into the Special Corps I wasn't even certain it really existed. It was too much like a con man's nightmare to be real. A secret worry. After a few happy years of successful crime you begin to wonder how long it will last. Planetary police are all pushovers and you start to feel you can go on forever if they're your only competition. What about the League though? Don't they take any interest in crime? Just about that time you hear your first rumor of the Special Corps and it fits the bad dreams. A shadowy, powerful group that slip silently between the stars, ready to bring the interstellar lawbreaker low. Sounds like TV drama stuff. I had been quite surprised to find they really existed.

I was even more surprised when I joined them. Of course there was a little pressure at the time. I had the alternative choice of instant death. But I still think it was a wise move. Under the motto "Set a thief to catch one," the Corps supposedly made good use of men like myself to get rid of the more antisocial types that infest the universe.

This was still all hearsay to me. I had been pulled into headquarters and given routine administration work for training. Six months of this had me slightly ga-ga and I wanted out. Since no one seemed to be in a hurry to give me an assignment I had found one for myself. I had no idea of what would come if it, but I also had no intention of returning until the job was done.

A quick stop at supply and record sections gave me everything I needed. The sun was barely clear of the horizon when the silver needle of my ship lifted in the gray field, then blasted into space.

The trip took only a few days, more than enough time to memorize everything I needed to know about Cittanuvo. And the more I knew the less I could understand their need for a battleship. It didn't fit. Cittanuvo was a secondary settlement out of the Cellini system, and I had run into these settlements before. They were all united in a loose alliance and bickered a lot among themselves, but never came to blows. If anything, they shared a universal abhorrence of war.

Yet they were secretly building a battleship.

Since I was only chasing my tail with this line of thought, I put it out of my mind and worked on some tri-di chess problems. This filled the time until Cittanuvo blinked into the bow screen.

One of my most effective mottoes has always been, "Secrecy can be an obviousity." What the magicians call misdirection. Let people very obviously see what you want them to see, then they'll never notice what is hidden. This was why I landed at midday, on the largest field on the planet, after a very showy approach. I was already dressed for my role, and out of the ship before the landing braces stopped vibrating. Buckling the fur cape around my shoulders with the platinum clasp, I stamped down the ramp. The sturdy little M-3 robot rumbled after me with my bags. Heading directly towards the main gate, I ignored the scurry of activity around the customs building. Only when a uniformed under-official of some kind ran over to me, did I give the field any attention.

Before he could talk I did, foot in the door and stay on top.

"Beautiful planet you have here. Delightful climate! Ideal spot for a country home. Friendly people, always willing to help strangers and all that I imagine. That's what I like. Makes me feel grateful. Very pleased to meet you. I am the Grand Duke Sant' Angelo." I shook his hand enthusiastically at this point and let a one hundred credit note slip into his palm.

"Now," I added, "I wonder if you would ask the customs agents to look at my bags here. Don't want to waste time, do we? The ship is open, they can check that whenever they please."

My manner, clothes, jewelry, the easy way I passed money around and the luxurious sheen of my bags, could mean only one thing. There was little that was worth smuggling into or out of Cittanuvo. Certainly nothing a rich man would be interested in. The official murmured something with a smile, spoke a few words into his phone, and the job was done.

A small wave of custom men hung stickers on my luggage, peeked into one or two for conformity's sake, and waved me through. I shook hands all around—a rustling hand-clasp of course—then was on my way. A cab was summoned, a hotel suggested. I nodded agreement and settled back while the robot loaded the bags about me.

*   *   *   *   *

The ship was completely clean. Everything I might need for the job was in my luggage. Some of it quite lethal and explosive, and very embarrassing if it was discovered in my bags. In the safety of my hotel suite I made a change of clothes and personality. After the robot had checked the rooms for bugs.

And very nice gadgets too, these Corps robots. It looked and acted like a moron M-3 all the time. It was anything but. The brain was as good as any other robot brain I have known, plus the fact that the chunky body was crammed with devices and machines of varying use. It chugged slowly around the room, moving my bags and laying out my kit. And all the time following a careful route that covered every inch of the suite. When it had finished it stopped and called the all-clear.

"All rooms checked. Results negative except for one optic bug in that wall."

"Should you be pointing like that?" I asked the robot. "Might make people suspicious, you know."

"Impossible," the robot said with mechanical surety. "I brushed against it and it is now unserviceable."

With this assurance I pulled off my flashy clothes and slipped into the midnight black dress uniform of an admiral in the League Grand Fleet. It came complete with decorations, gold bullion, and all the necessary documents. I thought it a little showy myself, but it was just the thing to make the right impression on Cittanuvo. Like many other planets, this one was uniform-conscious. Delivery boys, street cleaners, clerks—all had to have characteristic uniforms. Much prestige attached to them, and my black dress outfit should rate as high as any uniform in the galaxy.

A long cloak would conceal the uniform while I left the hotel, but the gold-encrusted helmet and a brief case of papers were a problem.

I had never explored all the possibilities of the pseudo M-3 robot, perhaps it could be of help.

"You there, short and chunky," I called. "Do you have any concealed compartments or drawers built into your steel hide? If so, let's see."

For a second I thought the robot had exploded. The thing had more drawers in it than a battery of cash registers. Big, small, flat, thin, they shot out on all sides. One held a gun and two more were stuffed with grenades; the rest were empty. I put the hat in one, the brief case in another and snapped my fingers. The drawers slid shut and its metal hide was as smooth as ever.

I pulled on a fancy sports cap, buckled the cape up tight, and was ready to go. The luggage was all booby-trapped and could defend itself. Guns, gas, poison needles, the usual sort of thing. In the last resort it would blow itself up. The M-3 went down by a freight elevator. I used a back stairs and we met in the street.

Since it was still daylight I didn't take a heli, but rented a groundcar instead. We had a leisurely drive out into the country and reached President Ferraro's house after dark.

As befitted the top official of a rich planet, the place was a mansion. But the security precautions were ludicrous to say the least. I took myself and a three hundred fifty kilo robot through the guards and alarms without causing the slightest stir. President Ferraro, a bachelor, was eating his dinner. This gave me enough undisturbed time to search his study.

There was absolutely nothing. Nothing to do with wars or battleships that is. If I had been interested in blackmail I had enough evidence in my hand to support me for life. I was looking for something bigger than political corruption, however.

When Ferraro rolled into his study after dinner the room was dark. I heard him murmur something about the servants and fumble for the switch. Before he found it, the robot closed the door and turned on the lights. I sat behind his desk, all his personal papers before me—weighted down with a pistol—and as fierce a scowl as I could raise smeared across my face. Before he got over the shock I snapped an order at him.

"Come over here and sit down, *quick!*"

The robot hustled him across the room at the same time, so he had no choice except to obey. When he saw the papers on the desk his eyes bulged and he just gurgled a little. Before he could recover I threw a thick folder in front of him.

"I am Admiral Thar, League Grand Fleet. These are my credentials. You had better check them." Since they were as good as any real admiral's I didn't worry in the slightest. Ferraro went through them as carefully as he could in his rattled state, even checking the seals under UV. It gave him time to regain a bit of control and he used it to bluster.

"What do you mean by entering my private quarters and burglaring—"

"You're in very bad trouble," I said in as gloomy a voice as I could muster.

Ferraro's tanned face went a dirty gray at my words. I pressed the advantage.

"I am arresting you for conspiracy, extortion, theft, and whatever other charges develop after a careful review of these documents. Seize him." This last order was directed at the robot who was well briefed in its role. It rumbled forward and locked its hand around Ferraro's wrist, handcuff style. He barely noticed.

"I can explain," he said desperately. "Everything can be explained. There is no need to make such charges. I don't know what papers you have there, so I wouldn't attempt to say they are all forgeries. I have many enemies you know. If the League knew the difficulties faced on a backward planet like this...."

"That will be entirely enough," I snapped, cutting him off with a wave of my hand. "All those questions will be answered by a court at the proper time. There is only one question I want an answer to now. Why are you building that battleship?"

   *   *   *   *   *

The man was a great actor. His eyes opened wide, his jaw dropped, he sank back into the chair as if he had been tapped lightly with a hammer. When he managed to speak the words were completely unnecessary; he had already registered every evidence of injured innocence.

"What battleship!" he gasped.

"The Warlord class battleship that is being built at the Cenerentola Spaceyards. Disguised behind these blueprints." I threw them across the desk to him, and pointed to one corner. "Those are your initials there, authorizing construction."

Ferraro still had the baffled act going as he fumbled with the papers, examined the initials and such. I gave him plenty of time. He finally put them down, shaking his head.

"I know nothing about any battleship. These are the plans for a new cargo liner. Those are my initials, I recall putting them there."

I phrased my question carefully, as I had him right where I wanted him now. "You deny any knowledge of the Warlord battleship that is being built from these modified plans."

"These are the plans for an ordinary passenger-freighter, that is all I know."

His words had the simple innocence of a young child's. Was he ever caught. I sat back with a relaxed sigh and lit a cigar.

"Wouldn't you be interested in knowing something about that robot who is holding you," I said. He looked down, as if aware for the first time that the robot had been holding him by the wrist during the interview. "That is no ordinary robot. It has a number of interesting devices built into its fingertips. Thermocouples, galvanometers, things like that. While you talked it registered your skin temperature, blood pressure, amount of perspiration and such. In other words it is an efficient and fast working lie detector. We will now hear all about your lies."

Ferraro pulled away from the robot's hand as if it had been a poisonous snake. I blew a relaxed smoke ring. "Report," I said to the robot. "Has this man told any lies?"

"Many," the robot said. "Exactly seventy-four per cent of all statements he made were fake."

"Very good," I nodded, throwing the last lock on my trap. "That means he knows all about this battleship."

"The subject has no knowledge of the battleship," the robot said coldly. "All of his statements concerning the construction of this ship were true."

Now it was my turn for the gaping and eye-popping act while Ferraro pulled himself together. He had no idea I wasn't interested in his other hanky-panky, but could tell I had had a low blow. It took an effort, but I managed to get my mind back into gear and consider the evidence.

If President Ferraro didn't know about the battleship, he must have been taken in by the cover-up job. But if he wasn't responsible—who was? Some militaristic clique that meant to overthrow him and take power? I didn't know enough about the planet, so I enlisted Ferraro on my side.

This was easy—even without the threat of exposure of the documents I had found in his files. Using their disclosure as a prod I could have made him jump through hoops. It wasn't necessary. As soon as I showed him the different blueprints and explained the possibilities he understood. If anything, he was more eager than I was to find out who was using his administration as a cat's-paw. By silent agreement the documents were forgotten.

We agreed that the next logical step would be the Cenerentola Spaceyards. He had some idea of sniffing around quietly first, trying to get a line to his political opponents. I gave him to understand that the League, and the League Navy in particular, wanted to stop the construction of the battleship. After that he could play his politics. With this point understood he called his car and squadron of guards and we made a parade to the shipyards. It was a four-hour drive and we made plans on the way down.

* * * * *

The spaceyard manager was named Rocca, and he was happily asleep when we arrived. But not for long. The parade of uniforms and guns in the middle of the night had him frightened into a state where he could hardly walk. I imagine he was as full of petty larceny as Ferraro. No innocent man could have looked so terror stricken. Taking advantage of the situation, I latched my motorized lie detector onto him and began snapping the questions.

Even before I had all the answers I began to get the drift of things. They were a little frightening, too. The manager of the spaceyard that was building the ship had no idea of its true nature.

Anyone with less self-esteem than myself—or who had led a more honest early life—might have doubted his own reasoning at that moment. I didn't. The ship on the ways *still* resembled a warship to six places. And knowing human nature the way I do, that was too much of a coincidence to expect. Occam's razor always points the way. If there are two choices to take, take the simpler. In this case I chose the natural acquisitive instinct of man as opposed to blind chance and accident. Nevertheless I put the theory to the test.

Looking over the original blueprints again, the big superstructure hit my eye. In order to turn the ship into a warship that would have to be one of the first things to go.

"Rocca!" I barked, in what I hoped was authentic old space-dog manner. "Look at these plans, at this space-going front porch here. Is it still being built onto the ship?"

He shook his head at once and said, "No, the plans were changed. We had to fit in some kind of new meteor-repelling gear for operating in the planetary debris belt."

I flipped through my case and drew out a plan. "Does your new gear look anything like this?" I asked, throwing it across the table to him.

He rubbed his jaw while he looked at it. "Well," he said hesitatingly, "I don't want to say for certain. After all these details aren't in my department, I'm just responsible for final assembly, not unit work. But this surely looks like the thing they installed. Big thing. Lots of power leads—"

It was a battleship all right, no doubt of that now. I was mentally reaching around to pat myself on the back when the meaning of his words sank in.

"Installed!" I shouted. "Did you say installed?"

Rocca collapsed away from my roar and gnawed his nails. "Yes—" he said, "not too long ago. I remember there was some trouble...."

"And what else!" I interrupted him. Cold moisture was beginning to collect along my spine now. "The drives, controls—are they in, too?"

"Why, yes," he said. "How did you know? The normal scheduling was changed around, causing a great deal of unnecessary trouble."

The cold sweat was now a running river of fear. I was beginning to have the feeling that I had been missing the boat all along the line. The original estimated date of completion was nearly a year away. But there was no real reason why that couldn't be changed, too.

"Cars! Guns!" I bellowed. "To the spaceyard. If that ship is anywhere near completion, we are in big, *big* trouble!"

      *   *   *   *   *

All the bored guards had a great time with the sirens, lights, accelerators on the floor and that sort of thing. We blasted a screaming hole through the night right to the spaceyard and through the gate.

It didn't make any difference, we were still too late. A uniformed watchman frantically waved to us and the whole convoy jerked to a stop.

The ship was gone.

Rocca couldn't believe it, neither could the president. They wandered up and down the empty ways where it had been built. I just crunched down in the back of the car, chewing my cigar to pieces and cursing myself for being a fool.

I had missed the obvious fact, being carried away by the thought of a planetary government building a warship. The government was involved for sure—but only as a pawn. No little planet-bound political mind could have dreamed up as big a scheme as this. I smelled a rat—a stainless steel one. Someone who operated the way I had done before my conversion.

Now that the rodent was well out of the bag I knew just where to look, and had a pretty good idea of what I would find. Rocca, the spaceyard manager, had staggered back and was pulling at his hair, cursing and crying at the same time. President Ferraro had his gun out and was staring at it grimly. It was hard to tell if he was thinking of murder or suicide. I didn't care which. All he had to worry about was the next election, when the voters and the political competition would carve him up for losing the ship. My troubles were a little bigger.

I had to find the battleship before it blasted its way across the galaxy.

"Rocca!" I shouted. "Get into the car. I want to see your records—*all* of your records—and I want to see them right now."

He climbed wearily in and had directed the driver before he fully realized what was happening. Blinking at the sickly light of dawn brought him slowly back to reality.

"But ... admiral ... the hour! Everyone will be asleep...."

I just growled, but it was enough. Rocca caught the idea from my expression and grabbed the car phone. The office doors were open when we got there.

Normally I curse the paper tangles of bureaucracy, but this was one time when I blessed them all. These people had it down to a fine science. Not a rivet fell, but that its fall was noted—in quintuplicate. And later followed up with a memo, *rivet, wastage, query*. The facts I needed were all neatly tucked away in their paper catacombs. All I had to do was sniff them out. I didn't try to look for first causes, this would have taken too long. Instead I concentrated my attention on the recent modifications, like the gun turret, that would quickly give me a trail to the guilty parties.

Once the clerks understood what I had in mind they hurled themselves into their work, urged on by the fires of patriotism and the burning voices of their superiors. All I had to do was suggest a line of search and the relevant documents would begin appearing at once.

*   *   *   *   *

Bit by bit a pattern started to emerge. A delicate webwork of forgery, bribery, chicanery and falsehood. It could only have been conceived by a mind as brilliantly crooked as my own. I chewed my lip with jealousy. Like all great ideas, this one was basically simple.

A party or parties unknown had neatly warped the ship construction program to their own ends. Undoubtedly they had started the program for the giant transport, that would have to be checked later. And once the program was underway, it had been guided with a skill that bordered on genius. Orders were originated in many places, passed on, changed and shuffled. I painfully traced each one to its source. Many times the source was a forgery. Some changes seemed to be unexplainable, until I noticed the officers in question had a temporary secretary while their normal assistants were ill. All the girls had food poisoning, a regular epidemic it seemed. Each of them in turn had been replaced by the same girl. She stayed just long enough in each position to see that the battleship plan moved forward one more notch.

This girl was obviously the assistant to the Mastermind who originated the scheme. He sat in the center of the plot, like a spider on its web, pulling the strings that set things into motion. My first thought that a gang was involved proved wrong. All my secondary suspects turned out to be simple forgeries, not individuals. In the few cases where forgery wasn't adequate, my mysterious X had apparently hired himself to do the job. X himself had the permanent job of Assistant Engineering Designer. One by one the untangled threads ran to this office. He also had a secretary whose "illnesses" coincided with her employment in other offices.

When I straightened up from my desk the ache in my back stabbed like a hot wire. I swallowed a painkiller and looked around at my drooping, sack-eyed assistants who had shared the sleepless seventy-two hour task. They sat or slumped against the furniture, waiting for my conclusions. Even President Ferraro was there, his hair looking scraggly where he had pulled out handfuls.

"You've found them, the criminal ring?" he asked, his fingers groping over his scalp for a fresh hold.

"I have found them, yes," I said hoarsely. "But not a criminal ring. An inspired master criminal—who apparently has more executive ability in one ear lobe than all your bribe-bloated bureaucrats—and his female assistant. They pulled the entire job by themselves. His name, or undoubtedly pseudoname, is Pepe Nero. The girl is called Angelina...."

"Arrest them at once! Guards ... guards—" Ferraro's voice died away as he ran out of the room. I talked to his vanishing back.

"That is just what we intend to do, but it's a little difficult at the moment since they are the ones who not only built the battleship, but undoubtedly stole it as well. It was fully automated so no crew is necessary."

"What do you plan to do?" one of the clerks asked.

"I shall do nothing," I told him, with the snapped precision of an old space dog. "The League fleet is already closing in on the renegades and you will be informed of the capture. Thank you for your assistance."

*   *   *   *   *

I threw them as snappy a salute as I could muster and they filed out. Staring gloomily at their backs I envied for one moment their simple faith in the League Navy. When in reality the vengeful fleet was just as imaginary as my admiral's rating. This was still a job for the Corps. Inskipp would have to be given the latest information at once. I had sent him a psigram about the theft, but there was no answer as yet. Maybe the identity of the thieves would stir some response out of him.

My message was in code, but it could be quickly broken if someone wanted to try hard enough. I took it to the message center myself. The psiman was in his transparent cubicle and I locked myself in with him. His eyes were unfocused as he spoke softly into a mike, pulling in a message from somewhere across the galaxy. Outside the rushing transcribers copied, coded and filed messages, but no sound penetrated the insulated wall. I waited until his attention clicked back into the room, and handed him the sheets of paper.

"League Central 14—rush," I told him.

He raised his eyebrows, but didn't ask any questions. Establishing contact only took a few seconds, as they had an entire battery of psimen for their communications. He read the code words carefully, shaping them with his mouth but not speaking aloud, the power of his thoughts carrying across the light-years of distance. As soon as he was finished I took back the sheet, tore it up and pocketed the pieces.

I had my answer back quickly enough, Inskipp must have been hovering around waiting for my message. The mike was turned off to the transcribers outside, and I took the code groups down in shorthand myself.

"... xybb dfil fdno, and if you don't—don't come back!"

The message broke into clear at the end and the psiman smiled as he spoke the words. I broke the point off my stylus and growled at him not to repeat *any* of this message, as it was classified, and I would personally see him shot if he did. That got rid of the smile, but didn't make me feel any better.

The decoded message turned out not to be as bad as I had imagined. Until further notice I was in charge of tracking and capturing the stolen battleship. I could call on the League for any aid I needed. I would keep my identity as an admiral for the rest of the job. I was to keep him informed of progress. Only those ominous last words in clear kept my happiness from being complete.

I had been handed my long-awaited assignment. But translated into simple terms my orders were to get the battleship, or it would be my neck. Never a word about my efforts in uncovering the plot in the first place. This is a heartless world we live in.

This moment of self-pity relaxed me and I immediately went to bed. Since my main job now was waiting, I could wait just as well asleep.

*   *   *   *   *

And waiting was all I could do. Of course there were secondary tasks, such as ordering a Naval cruiser for my own use, and digging for more information on the thieves, but these really were secondary to my main purpose. Which was waiting for bad news. There was no place I could go that would be better situated for the chase than Cittanuvo. The missing ship could have gone in any direction. With each passing minute the sphere of probable locations grew larger by the power of the squared cube. I kept the on-watch crew of the cruiser at duty stations and confined the rest within a one hundred yard radius of the ship.

There was little more information on Pepe and Angelina, they had covered their tracks well. Their origin was unknown, though the fact they both talked with a slight accent suggested an off-world origin. There was one dim picture of Pepe, chubby but looking too grim to be a happy fat boy. There was no picture of the girl. I shuffled the meager findings, controlled my impatience, and kept the ship's psiman busy pulling in all the reports of any kind of trouble in space. The navigator and I plotted their locations in his tank, comparing the positions in relation to the growing sphere that enclosed all the possible locations of the stolen ship. Some of the disasters and apparent accidents hit inside this area, but further investigation proved them all to have natural causes.

I had left standing orders that all reports falling inside the danger area were to be brought to me at any time. The messenger woke me from a deep sleep, turning on the light and handing me the slip of paper. I blinked myself awake, read the first two lines, and pressed the *action station* alarm over my bunk. I'll say this, the Navy boys know their business. When the sirens screamed, the crew secured ship and blasted off before I had finished reading the report. As soon as my eyeballs unsquashed back into focus I read it through, then once more, carefully, from the beginning.

It looked like the one we had been waiting for. There were no witnesses to the tragedy, but a number of monitor stations had picked up the discharge static of a large energy weapon being fired. Triangulation had lead investigators to the spot where they found a freighter, *Ogget's Dream*, with a hole punched through it as big as a railroad tunnel. The freighter's cargo of plutonium was gone.

I read *Pepe* in every line of the message. Since he was flying an undermanned battleship, he had used it in the most efficient way possible. If he attempted to negotiate or threaten another ship, the element of chance would be introduced. So he had simply roared up to the unsuspecting freighter and blasted her with the monster guns his battleship packed. All eighteen men aboard had been killed instantly. The thieves were now murderers.

I was under pressure now to act. And under a greater pressure not to make any mistakes. Roly-poly Pepe had shown himself to be a ruthless killer. He knew what he wanted—then reached out and took it. Destroying anyone who stood in his way. More people would die before this was over, it was up to me to keep that number as small as possible.

     *   *   *   *   *

Ideally I should have rushed out the fleet with guns blazing and dragged him to justice. Very nice, and I wished it could be done that way. Except where was he? A battleship may be gigantic on some terms of reference, but in the immensity of the galaxy it is microscopically infinitesimal. As long as it stayed out of the regular lanes of commerce, and clear of detector stations and planets, it would never be found.

Then how *could* I find it—and having found it, catch it? When the infernal thing was more than a match for any ship it might meet. That was my problem. It had kept me awake nights and talking to myself days, since there was no easy answer.

I had to construct a solution, slowly and carefully. Since I couldn't be sure where Pepe was going to be next, I had to make him go where I wanted him to.

There were some things in my favor. The most important was the fact I had forced him to make his play before he was absolutely ready. It wasn't chance that he had left the same day I arrived on Cittanuvo. Any plan as elaborate as his certainly included warning of approaching danger. The drive on the battleship, as well as controls and primary armament had been installed weeks before I showed up. Much of the subsidiary work remained to be done when the ship had left. One witness of the theft had graphically described the power lines and cables dangling from the ship's locks when she lifted.

My arrival had forced Pepe off balance. Now I had to keep pushing until he fell. This meant I had to think as he did, fall into his plan, think ahead—then trap him. Set a thief to catch a thief. A great theory, only I felt uncomfortably on the spot when I tried to put it into practice.

A drink helped, as did a cigar. Puffing on it, staring at the smooth bulkhead, relaxed me a bit. After all—there aren't that many things you can do with a battleship. You can't run a big con, blow safes or make burmedex with it. It is hell-on-jets for space piracy, but that's about all.

"Great, great—but why a battleship?"

I was talking to myself, normally a bad sign, but right now I didn't care. The mood of space piracy had seized me and I had been going along fine. Until this glaring inconsistency jumped out and hit me square in the eye.

Why a battleship? Why all the trouble and years of work to get a ship that two people could just barely manage? With a tenth of the effort Pepe could have had a cruiser that would have suited his purposes just as well.

Just as good for space piracy, that is—but not for *his* purposes. He had wanted a battleship, and he had gotten himself a battleship. Which meant he had more in mind than simple piracy. What? It was obvious that Pepe was a monomaniac, an egomaniac, and as psychotic as a shorted computer. Some day the mystery of how he had slipped through the screen of official testing would have to be investigated. That wasn't my concern now. He still had to be caught.

*   *   *   *   *

A plan was beginning to take shape in my head, but I didn't rush it. First I had to be sure that I knew him well. Any man that can con an entire world into building a battleship for him—then steal it from them—is not going to stop there. The ship would need a crew, a base for refueling and a mission.

Fuel had been taken care of first, the gutted hull of *Ogget's Dream* was silent witness to that. There were countless planets that could be used as a base. Getting a crew would be more difficult in these peaceful times, although I could think of a few answers to that one, too. Raid the mental hospitals and jails. Do that often enough and you would have a crew that would make any pirate chief proud.

Though piracy was, of course, too mean an ambition to ascribe to this boy. Did he want to rule a whole planet—or maybe an entire system? Or more? I shuddered a bit as the thought hit me. Was there really anything that could stop a plan like this once it got rolling? During the Kingly Wars any number of types with a couple of ships and less brains than Pepe had set up just this kind of empire. They were all pulled down in the end, since their success depended on one-man rule. But the price that had to be paid first!

This was the plan and I felt in my bones that I was right. I might be wrong on some of the minor details, they weren't important. I knew the general outline of the idea, just as when I bumped into a mark I knew how much he could be taken for, and just how to do it. There are natural laws in crime as in every other field of human endeavor. I *knew* this was it.

"Get the Communications Officer in here at once," I shouted at the intercom. "Also a couple of clerks with transcribers. And fast—this is a matter of life or death!" This last had a hollow ring, and I realized my enthusiasm had carried me out of character. I buttoned my collar, straightened my ribbons and squared my shoulders. By the time they knocked on the door I was all admiral again.

Acting on my orders the ship dropped out of warpdrive so our psiman could get through to the other operators. Captain Steng grumbled as we floated there with the engines silent, wasting precious days, while half his crew was involved in getting out what appeared to be insane instructions. My plan was beyond his understanding. Which is, of course, why he is a captain and I'm an admiral, even a temporary one.

Following my orders, the navigator again constructed a sphere of speculation in his tank. The surface of the sphere contacted all the star systems a days flight ahead of the maximum flight of the stolen battleship. There weren't too many of these at first and the psiman could handle them all, calling each in turn and sending by news releases to the Naval Public Relations officers there. As the sphere kept growing he started to drop behind, steadily losing ground. By this time I had a general release prepared, along with directions for use and follow up, which he sent to Central 14. The battery of

psimen there contacted the individual planets and all we had to do
was keep adding to the list of planets.

The release and follow-ups all harped on one theme. I expanded on
it, waxed enthusiastic, condemned it, and worked it into an
interview. I wrote as many variations as I could, so it could be slipped
into as many different formats as possible. In one form or another I
wanted the basic information in every magazine, newspaper and
journal inside that expanding sphere.

"What in the devil does this nonsense *mean?*" Captain Steng asked
peevishly. He had long since given up the entire operation as a futile
one, and spent most of the time in his cabin worrying about the
affect of it on his service record. Boredom or curiosity had driven him
out, and he was reading one of my releases with horror.

"Billionaire to found own world ... space yacht filled with luxuries
to last a hundred years," the captain's face grew red as he flipped
through the stack of notes. "What connection does this tripe have
with catching those murderers?"

    *   *   *   *   *

When we were alone he was anything but courteous to me, having
assured himself by not-too-subtle questioning that I was a spurious
admiral. There was no doubt I was still in charge, but our relationship
was anything but formal.

"This tripe and nonsense," I told him, "is the bait that will snag
our fish. A trap for Pepe and his partner in crime."

"Who is this mysterious billionaire?"

"Me," I said. "I've always wanted to be rich."

"But this ship, the space yacht, where is it?"

"Being built now in the naval shipyard at Udrydde. We're almost
ready to go there now, soon as this batch of instructions goes out."

Captain Steng dropped the releases onto the table, then carefully
wiped his hands off to remove any possible infection. He was trying
to be fair and considerate of my views, and not succeeding in the
slightest.

"It doesn't make sense," he growled. "How can you be sure this
killer will ever read one of these things. And if he does—why should
he be interested? It looks to me as if you are wasting time while he
slips through your fingers. The alarm should be out and every ship
notified. The Navy alerted and patrols set on all spacelanes—"

"Which he could easily avoid by going around, or better yet not even bother about, since he can lick any ship we have. That's not the answer," I told him. "This Pepe is smart and as tricky as a fixed gambling machine. That's his strength—and his weakness as well. Characters like that never think it possible for someone else to outthink them. Which is what *I'm* going to do."

"Modest, aren't you," Steng said.

"I try not to be," I told him. "False modesty is the refuge of the incompetent. I'm going to catch this thug and I'll tell you how I'll do it. He's going to hit again soon, and wherever he hits there will be some kind of a periodical with my plant in it. Whatever else he is after, he is going to take all of the magazines and papers he can find. Partly to satisfy his own ego, but mostly to keep track of the things he is interested in. Such as ship sailings."

"You're just guessing—you don't know all this."

His automatic assumption of my incompetence was beginning to get me annoyed. I bridled my temper and tried one last time.

"Yes, I'm guessing—an informed guess—but I do know some facts as well. *Ogget's Dream* was cleaned out of all reading matter, that was one of the first things I checked. We can't stop the battleship from attacking again, but we can see to it that the time after that she sails into a trap."

"I don't know," the captain said, "it sounds to me like...."

I never heard what it sounded like, which is all right since he was getting under my skin and might have been tempted to pull my pseudo-rank. The alarm sirens cut his sentence off and we foot-raced to the communications room.

Captain Steng won by a nose, it was his ship and he knew all the shortcuts. The psiman was holding out a transcription, but he summed it up in one sentence. He looked at me while he talked and his face was hard and cold.

"They hit again, knocked out a Navy supply satellite, thirty-four men dead."

"If your plan doesn't work, *admiral*," the captain whispered hoarsely in my ear, "I'll personally see that you're flayed alive!"

"If my plan doesn't work, *captain*—there won't be enough of my skin left to pick up with a tweezer. Now if you please, I'd like to get to Udrydde and pick up my ship as soon as possible."

The easy-going hatred and contempt of all my associates had annoyed me, thrown me off balance. I was thinking with anger now, not with logic. Forcing a bit of control, I ordered my thoughts, checking off a mental list.

"Belay that last command," I shouted, getting back into my old space-dog mood. "Get a call through first and find out if any of our plants were picked up during the raid."

While the psiman unfocused his eyes and mumbled under his breath I riffled some papers, relaxed and cool. The ratings and officers waited tensely, and made some slight attempt to conceal their hatred of me. It took about ten minutes to get an answer.

"Affirmative," the psiman said. "A store ship docked there twenty hours before the attack. Among other things, it left newspapers containing the article."

"Very good," I said calmly. "Send a general order to suspend all future activity with the planted releases. Send it by psimen only, no mention on any other Naval signaling equipment, there's a good chance now it might be 'overheard.'"

I strolled out slowly, in command of the situation. Keeping my face turned away so they couldn't see the cold sweat.

*　*　*　*　*

It was a fast run to Udrydde where my billionaire's yacht, the *Eldorado*, was waiting. The dockyard commander showed me the ship, and made a noble effort to control his curiosity. I took a sadistic revenge on the Navy by not telling him a word about my mission. After checking out the controls and special apparatus with the technicians, I cleared the ship. There was a tape in the automatic navigator that would put me on the course mentioned in all the articles, just a press of a button and I would be on my way. I pressed the button.

It was a beautiful ship, and the dockyard had been lavish with their attention to detail. From bow to rear tubes she was plated in pure gold. There are other metals with a higher albedo, but none that give a richer effect. All the fittings, inside and out, were either machine-turned or plated. All this work could not have been done in the time allotted, the Navy must have adapted a luxury yacht to my needs.

Everything was ready. Either Pepe would make his move—or I would sail on to my billionaire's paradise planet. If that happened, it would be best if I stayed there.

Now that I was in space, past the point of no return, all the doubts that I had dismissed fought for attention. The plan that had seemed so clear and logical now began to look like a patched and crazy makeshift.

"Hold on there, sailor," I said to myself. Using my best admiral's voice. "Nothing has changed. It's still the best and *only* plan possible under the circumstances."

Was it? Could I be sure that Pepe, flying his mountain of a ship and eating Navy rations, would be interested in some of the comforts and luxuries of life? Or if the luxuries didn't catch his eye, would he be interested in the planetary homesteading gear? I had loaded the cards with all the things he might want, and planted the information where he could get it. He had the bait now—but would he grab the hook?

I couldn't tell. And I could work myself into a neurotic state if I kept running through the worry cycle. It took an effort to concentrate on anything else, but it had to be made. The next four days passed very slowly.

When the alarm blew off, all I felt was an intense sensation of relief. I might be dead and blasted to dust in the next few minutes, but that didn't seem to make much difference.

Pepe had swallowed the bait. There was only one ship in the galaxy that could knock back a blip that big at such a distance. It was closing fast, using the raw energy of the battleship engines for a headlong approach. My ship bucked a bit as the tug-beams locked on at maximum distance. The radio bleeped at me for attention at the same time. I waited as long as I dared, then flipped it on. The voice boomed out.

"... That you are under the guns of a warship! Don't attempt to run, signal, take evasive action, or in any other way...."

"Who are you—and what the devil do you want?" I spluttered into the mike. I had my scanner on, so they could see me, but my own screen stayed dark. They weren't sending any picture. In a way it made my act easier, I just played to an unseen audience. They could see the rich cut of my clothes, the luxurious cabin behind me. Of course they couldn't see my hands.

"It doesn't matter who we are," the radio boomed again. "Just obey orders if you care to live. Stay away from the controls until we have tied on, then do exactly as I say."

There were two distant clangs as magnetic grapples hit the hull. A little later the ship lurched, drawn home against the battleship. I let my eyes roll in fear, looking around for a way to escape—and taking a peek at the outside scanners. The yacht was flush against the space-filling bulk of the other ship. I pressed the button that sent the torch-wielding robot on his way.

* * * * *

"Now let me tell you something," I snapped into the mike, wiping away the worried billionaire expression. "First I'll repeat your own warning—obey orders if you want to live. I'll show you why—"

When I threw the big switch a carefully worked out sequence took place. First, of course, the hull was magnetized and the bombs fused. A light blinked as the scanner in the cabin turned off, and the one in the generator room came on. I checked the monitor screen to make sure, then started into the spacesuit. It had to be done fast, at the same time it was necessary to talk naturally. They must still think of me as sitting in the control room.

"That's the ship's generators you're looking at," I said. "Ninety-eight per cent of their output is now feeding into coils that make an electromagnet of this ship's hull. You will find it very hard to separate us. And I would advise you not to try."

The suit was on, and I kept the running chatter up through the mike in the helmet, relaying to the ship's transmitter. The scene in the monitor receiver changed.

"You are now looking at a hydrogen bomb that is primed and aware of the magnetic field holding our ships together. It will, of course, go off if you try to pull away."

I grabbed up the monitor receiver and ran towards the air lock.

"This is a different bomb now," I said, keeping one eye on the screen and the other on the slowly opening outer door. "This one has receptors on the hull. Attempt to destroy any part of this ship, or even gain entry to it, and this one will detonate."

I was in space now, leaping across to the gigantic wall of the other ship.

"What do you want?" These were the first words Pepe had spoken since his first threats.

"I want to talk to you, arrange a deal. Something that would be profitable for both of us. But let me first show you the rest of the bombs, so you won't get any strange ideas about co-operating."

Of course I *had* to show him the rest of the bombs, there was no getting out of it. The scanners in the ship were following a planned program. I made light talk about all my massive armament that would carry us both to perdition, while I climbed through the hole in the battleship's hull. There was no armor or warning devices at this spot, it had been chosen carefully from the blueprints.

"Yeah, yeah ... I take your word for it, you're a flying bomb. So stop with this roving reporter bit and tell me what you have in mind."

This time I didn't answer him, because I was running and panting like a dog, and had the mike turned off. Just ahead, if the blueprints were right, was the door to the control room. Pepe should be there.

I stepped through, gun out, and pointed it at the back of his head. Angelina stood next to him, looking at the screen.

"The game's over," I said. "Stand up slowly and keep your hands in sight."

"What do you mean," he said angrily, looking at the screen in front of him. The girl caught wise first. She spun around and pointed.

"He's *here!*"

They both stared, gaped at me, caught off guard and completely unprepared.

"You're under arrest, crime-king," I told him. "And your girl friend."

Angelina rolled her eyes up and slid slowly to the floor. Real or faked, I didn't care. I kept the gun on Pepe's pudgy form while he picked her up and carried her to an acceleration couch against the wall.

"What ... what will happen now?" He quavered the question. His pouchy jaws shook and I swear there were tears in his eyes. I was not impressed by his acting since I could clearly remember the dead men floating in space. He stumbled over to a chair, half dropping into it.

"Will they do anything to me?" Angelina asked. Her eyes were open now.

"I have no idea of what will happen to you," I told her truthfully. "That is up to the courts to decide."

"But he *made* me do all those things," she wailed. She was young, dark and beautiful, the tears did nothing to spoil this.

Pepe dropped his face into his hands and his shoulders shook. I flicked the gun his way and snapped at him.

"Sit up, Pepe. I find it very hard to believe that you are crying. There are some Naval ships on the way now, the automatic alarm was triggered about a minute ago. I'm sure they'll be glad to see the man who...."

"Don't let them take me, please!" Angelina was on her feet now, her back pressed to the wall. "They'll put me in prison, do things to my mind!" She shrunk away as she spoke, stumbling along the wall. I looked back at Pepe, not wanting to have my eyes off him for an instant.

"There's nothing I can do," I told her. I glanced her way and a small door was swinging open and she was gone.

"Don't try to run," I shouted after her, "it can't do any good!"

Pepe made a strangling noise and I looked back to him quickly. He was sitting up now and his face was dry of tears. In fact he was laughing, not crying.

"So she caught you, too, Mr. Wise-cop, poor little Angelina with the soft eyes." He broke down again, shaking with laughter.

"What do you mean," I growled.

"Don't you catch yet? The story she told you was true—except she twisted it around a bit. The whole plan, building the battleship, then stealing it, was *hers*. She pulled me into it, played me like an accordion. I fell in love with her, hating myself and happy at the same time. Well—I'm glad now it's over. At least I gave her a chance to get away, I owe her that much. Though I thought I would explode when she went into that innocence act!"

The cold feeling was now a ball of ice that threatened to paralyze me. "You're lying," I said hoarsely, and even I didn't believe it.

"Sorry. That's the way it is. Your brain-boys will pick my skull to pieces and find out the truth anyway. There's no point in lying now."

"We'll search the ship, she can't hide for long."

"She won't have to," Pepe said. "There's a fast scout we picked up, stowed in one of the holds. That must be it leaving now." We could feel the vibration, distantly through the floor.

"The Navy will get her," I told him, with far more conviction than I felt.

"Maybe," he said, suddenly slumped and tired, no longer laughing. "Maybe they will. But I gave her her chance. It is all over for me now, but she knows that I loved her to the end." He bared his teeth in sudden pain. "Not that she will care in the slightest."

I kept the gun on him and neither of us moved while the Navy ships pulled up and their boots stamped outside. I had captured my battleship and the raids were over. And I couldn't be blamed if the girl had slipped away. If she evaded the Navy ships, that was their fault, not mine.

I had my victory all right.

Then why did it taste like ashes in my mouth?

It's a big galaxy, but it wasn't going to be big enough to hide Angelina now. I can be conned once—but only once. The next time we met things were going to be *very* different.

CPSIA information can be obtained
at www.ICGtesting.com
Printed in the USA
BVHW030845200322
631671BV00004B/627